BETTY'S HAT
Collection of
Short Stories and Verses

J. D. Willis

GW00600846

ARTHUR H. STOCKWELL LTD.
Elms Court   Ilfracombe   Devon
Established 1898

British Library Cataloguing-in-Publication Data.
A catalogue record for this book is available
from the British Library.

ISBN 0 7223 3090-1

Printed in Great Britain by
Arthur H. Stockwell Ltd.
Elms Court   Ilfracombe
Devon

CONTENTS

To / Sue & family from. Dave

SUMMER DAY

Sitting on the bank of the river, watching the willow dip its leaves in the water, disturbing the flow of the river as it travels on its way. Once in a while, fish would break the surface, catching insects which had fallen in the water or landed. On these summer days, everything seems to be enjoying life. Reed bunting flying backwards and forwards feeding their young, never seemingly to tire with the demand. The kingfisher appears from nowhere with a small fish in its beak, turning it sideways to swallow. Across the field the cows are grazing, soaking up sun as they go, disturbing the wildlife and insects; some birds, seizing the opportunity for an easy meal, making life easy for some. Watching the water lilies bobbing up and down in time with the water. Dragonflies trying to settle on the bobbing lilies, enjoying their short life.

In the distance a tractor was edging its way towards me. As it got near, the farmer nodded to me. I nodded back. He said,

"Can't you read? 'PRIVATE PROPERTY'!"

FRIENDSHIP

The garden was full of flowers; an assortment of hollyhocks dotted the back of the borders. Marguerites, with their lovely white tops standing out among the lupins. Lupins were just coming to the end of their term of flowering. A larger group of foxgloves were just coming into flower. Small marigolds were planted along the full length of the border. At the back, a wild honeysuckle had woven itself along the fence. A path made its way down the garden, stopping just short of a large oak tree. Lily had planted the acorn when she had first moved in, some fifty years ago.

The garden was beginning to show signs of neglect. Lily had tried her best to keep it neat and tidy. But at seventy-two years old it was becoming very difficult and hard for her to keep the garden under control. Her husband had passed away some years earlier; both of them had always enjoyed looking after the garden, and attending to its occupants, at the same time enjoying the pleasure it gave them.

As she sat in her garden awaiting the arrival of her grandchildren, she hoped her new neighbours would turn out to be nice people. They had moved in some weeks earlier. She had not seen them to speak to.

The grandchildren come around most Sundays to see her and play in the garden. On arrival, they would kiss and cuddle her and then run straight into the garden to play around the oak tree. The children loved the tree because they could climb up it and swing on the rope that was attached to one of the many branches. The tree, at times, seemed to be looking after Lily and her family; standing tall and proud, with open arms, inviting the children to play around it. At the same time giving Lily some shade whenever she sat in her garden.

As the months went by, Lily got to know her new neighbours. At first they seemed nice, but slowly they started to complain about the state of the fence, plus the weeds growing through to their side. Lily started to worry and get concerned about the state of her garden. The next time they complained, it was about the tree being too big and blocking out their light with its large branches, which overhung their property. Lily knew she could not do anything about the tree, but she tried to mend the fence the best way she could, pulling out some of the weeds as she went along.

Slowly Lily stopped going into her garden; the grandchildren stopped playing around their favourite tree. A sadness had fallen upon the garden, all because of the neighbours.

Looking out of her window one morning, Lily noticed her neighbour had placed a ladder against the tree. It seemed the neighbour had taken it upon himself to cut off the overhanging branches. Just as he reached the top of the ladder and began to saw through the branch, the tree seemed to sway and move for no apparent reason, causing him to lose his grip, dropping the saw. The ladder slid away from the branch he had hoped to cut down. As he was clinging to his only hope of survival with all his strength, the tree started to sway and move once again causing him to lose his hold and fall to the ground with a thud and a cracking sound in his leg. This causing him to have at least six months off work.

Having so much time off, caused him financial problems, resulting in him having to sell the house.

The new neighbours were quite nice; they told Lily, how when they came to view the house, one of the things that they liked was the garden and the big oak tree in her garden. Lily was happy they liked her tree; she could once again sit in her beloved garden with her memories, and her grandchildren once again play around their favourite tree, swinging on the rope enjoying themselves.

Lily's eyes looked up at the tree, it seemed to be swaying gently to and fro. She smiled to herself; deep down she knew the old oak was looking after her and the children, as she had looked after the oak.

FLATFORD

The early-morning mist rising like a veil, releasing its hold upon the surface of the water; evaporating slowly, allowing the sun through. Creating a mystic feeling across the water, the sun's rays beginning to reflect off the dew still clinging to its host. Droplets of dew slowly vanishing, as the sun warms up the meadow. Scattered across the meadow, cowpats waiting patiently for an intruder.

At the water's edge, through the mist, a tall grey figure; a heron moving slowly, slyly stalking; suddenly, frogs' legs for breakfast. In the distance geese can be heard honking their way through the rising mist on the way to pastures new. Through the mist the willow appeared like a giant canopy above the water mill, with its long tentacles reaching down scratching the surface of the water. Coots gingerly weaving their way through the reeds, picking and poking at anything that catches their eyes, in their quest for survival. A swan gently glides the water, like an iceberg creating rings, as it drifts in the gentle breeze. Noisy, green mallard ducks, flying in, circling around and finally skimming to a halt on the millpond disturbing the gentle silence of the early morning.

Suddenly, a voice shouts out. I turn, WHOOPS, I found a cowpat.

"Can't you read? 'NO TRESPASSERS'!"

COTTAGE

She found herself looking out of the small leaded window of her cottage. The memory was coming back of the life she had spent in her beloved cottage. Through the window she could see the construction of the new motorway slowly edging ever nearer to her home. It would be only a matter of weeks before her home was destroyed. Her eyes welled up with sadness at the thought of what was happening. Her home was a small thatched cottage; to her knowledge at least a hundred years old.

When she had first arrived at the cottage, over fifty years ago, it was a cold and lonely place; no electricity, oil lamps for light and cooking. As the years went by, things improved, electricity came into her home. She and her husband worked hard over the years decorating, planting up their garden, growing their own vegetables.

She slowly fingered the locket which hung around her neck; a present from her husband on their wedding night. She looked at the fireplace, tears running down her cheeks. Her late husband's rocking chair still near the fireplace; just the right distance now, for when she was poking the fire. Smoke was still drifting up the chimney from the last remaining embers of the day. Remembering the long winter nights, when her children would make toast, roast chestnuts and laugh at the shadows they made on the wall in front of the fire, she slowly wiped away her tears with the bottom of her nightdress. Low wooden beams stretched across the ceiling and around the front door. She had lost count over the years, how many times people had knocked their head on the beams. Turning and glancing at her dresser, with its blue and white willow pattern china, and some of the family heirlooms, her tears started to run again.

Outside a white dog rose grew near the front door; along the side, a sweet-smelling honeysuckle clung to the red brick, reaching out to tap the window. In the back garden, hollyhocks grew tall against the cottage, their rosette flowers reaching up to touch the roof. Along the borders grew lupins, some red, others in blue; tall foxgloves peeking over the wooden fence; candytuft dotted along the edge, with some blue Canterbury bells adding more colour. All were interlaced along the border, making their way towards the gate. She knew their days were numbered, as well as her own. She wiped more tears away as she began to sob uncontrollably. Even the blackbirds who had brought up their family in the thatch would have to find a new home. It seemed to her the cottage with its old red brick, wooden beams, thatch roof, roses around the door, a garden full of colour and a welcoming gate, would be destroyed because of a new road. Faintly she heard the blackbird singing; slowly it got louder, its song waking her up; her face was wet, her hands were clammy.

She jumped up off the bed, and ran to the window pushing aside the lace curtain, throwing open the cottage window, realising it was all a nightmare. "That's the last time I eat cheese so late at night!" she cried.

BETTY'S HAT

Betty looked into the mirror, adjusting the new hat she had bought at a local boot sale a few weeks earlier. The hat made out of straw, with its wide brim, was just right for the summer, with the red ribbon she had placed around the top, adding a bit more colour.

As she closed her garden gate, Mrs Thomas at number 27 nodded and said "I like your hat." Betty smiled back.

Further along the avenue across the road, Mrs Kitson and her neighbour were chatting; they both looked across and smiled at Betty. "Nice hat" they said. Betty felt as proud as a peacock; her new hat was making people turn their heads. People were looking at her and smiling.

As she entered her local supermarket, the assistant smiled and said "Lovely hat Betty."

Going around the counters, picking up her weekly shopping, she spotted some lovely black grapes; advancing closer to them, she pulled one from the bunch to taste.

All of a sudden over the Tannoy, a voice said, "The lady in the big hat. Can't you read? Do not touch."

Betty looked up from under the wide brim, to see herself caught on the security video, embarrassed to see that the ticket was still on her hat; 25p.

KEITH

Keith sat there listening to the rain beating on the windows, as he finished his cup of tea. His mind started to think about the next "job".

Keith's wife had left for work as usual about eight-thirty that morning and would not return until about five that evening. Keith sat there rejoicing in the fact that he had got away with four post office raids, in as many months. Living close to the motorway enabled him to travel up and down the country, and make a quick getaway after doing the "job". Keith had lost his job as a salesman, about eighteen months before.

Sergeant Gray, at his local police station in Woofing, had advised him about joining the police force. With a clean driving record and a good character, he had applied to join. He had passed the exams and medical with flying colours and his references were good. While waiting to go in the force, he came up with the idea to rob sub-post offices. Straight down the motorway, and onto the country lanes and back again, before his wife came home from work.

He cleared the table of the breakfast things, so he could lay the map out and study the roads. He came across a small village, about forty miles away on the map. It would do nicely for the last "job" before his starting date comes to join the police. He recalled the village was small, and the post office was situated on the left-hand side as you enter; just right for parking and getting away quick.

He left about nine-forty on the Tuesday morning to do the "job". The journey did not take too long; straight down the motorway, following the signposts to the village. Once in the village he took care not to attract attention, driving at the right speed at all times. He parked outside the post office, got out of the car, and walked in placing himself in the queue. When he reached the counter, he produced a gun and then demanded the money. The cashier gave him the cash straightaway. Keith then ran out, got into the car and drove off. As he approached the traffic lights, they changed, making him accelerate and jump the lights. He was soon away, and down the country lanes, and home before his wife. By the time she got home, the tea was laid out.

Sitting there relaxing the following Saturday morning, he heard the postman dropping the mail through the letter box. His wife went and picked the letters up, handing him the one he had been waiting for, from the police. He eagerly opened the letter, hoping to see his starting date, but inside, was a picture of his car jumping the lights, plus the date and time with his registration number. He had been caught on the traffic camera. He looked at his wife open-mouthed.

"25, NOT OUT"

Making my way through the woods; trees, with their outstretched arms, forming a lovely cool canopy above, helping to catch the aroma of the undergrowth, the warm, musky, earthy smell that only comes from new growth and composting old. Ferns unrolling their new foliage for the coming summer, reaching upwards. Dark ivy climbing up, smothering everything as it goes. Blackbirds scratching and flicking the leaf mould over, with their yellow beaks.

Emerging onto the village green; moles having left their calling cards along the edge; just like the courting couple I just stumbled over. Giant oak trees and elms, looking down on the local cricket team. Swifts flying high soaring around; others flying low, skimming the mowed grass in the summer heat.

Making my way across the village green, feeling the lovely soft grass under my feet, as I went towards the local village fete, hoping my friend had maximum points for winning the cake decorating competition.

All of a sudden, people were shouting and waving to me. I smiled and waved back. I looked up — a cricket ball!

Ten minutes later when I came to, Dave the captain of the LMF cricket team said,

"Can't you read?

'KEEP OFF THE GRASS'!"

MAIDEN OVER

Having recovered sufficiently from the sudden appearance of a cricket ball, I thank Dave the captain for his help and advice in avoiding another six not out. Moving slowly towards the entrance to the tent, narrowly avoiding the guy rope as I went, I placed my foot in a bowl of water, placed there to refresh the dogs. I finally reached the tent where the cake competition was being held.

Cakes in the shapes of Superman, Postman Pat, animals and a magical friend, patiently and painstakingly decorated; all of them deserving a prize for imagination and skill. The vicar, with buck teeth, dog collar, cup of tea and a home-made scone, had just awarded first prize to Miss Eaves for her winning cake of a pair of leaping dolphins. Miss Eaves, in a floral dress, straw hat, summer sandals and a big smile, placed her certificate of award next to a display of wild flowers which were adding a bit more to the summer day.

Having edged my way towards the front, I suddenly tripped, knocking the table over, sending the winning cake flying; its final resting place my head. I looked up and licked my lips; everyone was peering down, smiling faces, angry faces, some bemused.

The vicar looked over; reaching down, he peeled a piece of the cake off my face. "Nice cake, pity you did not read the notice."

"MIND THE ROPE".

FINAL SCORE

I emerged from the confectionery tent with the vicar's voice still ringing in my ears, and the taste of the cake on my lips. Some families were making their way home; children with their white floppy hats were beginning to fall asleep in their pushchairs. People carrying plants, picnic baskets, and balloons trying hard to fly away, were slowly trailing across the green. Long tall shadows began to appear across the field as the sun set, throwing out its last rays of the day.

As I approached the pond, the summer evening was adding its own personal touch to the still waters. Gnats appeared at the water's edge, like dancing puppets with no strings. Last of the acrobatic swallows, skimmed the calm waters for supper. Grey geese cut a fine line across the still waters. White swans with their cygnets settling down for the night. "It was magic."

A willow leant over and tickled the surface of the water, and offered shelter to its evening residents. The quietness of the summer evening did help me to forget my black eye, soggy foot, but not the taste of that lovely cake. I turned and looked back at the cricket scoreboard; last players 51 and 47 not out. LMF team won.

WINDOW '95

The snow was falling silently and settled everywhere, gently coating everything, changing the scenery from green to white. Bullfinches, which once enjoyed the seeds and the view, gone. The teasel, with its prickly leaves, slowly being covered and bent by the falling snow, is now capped in white. The once green grass was slowly disappearing, now bent and broken withering away in the deepening drifting snow. A bare weeping willow peered down at the frozen water, looking sad and lonely, against a cold grey sky and the encroaching blizzard. Its only company, starlings clustered along its now bare branches, their feathers puffed up against the chilled wind and falling snow. Silver birches, their ghostly appearance etched against the snow-filled sky. Bulrushes and reads, having turned brown, prevented now from swaying in the wind, locked in the frozen ice, bending and breaking under the weight of the falling snow. Seagulls standing on frozen water, hunched and huddled up on one leg against the cold wind and driving snow.

Across the frozen ice, bewildered black coots lined the frozen water's edge, slowly turning white in the falling snow, unable to feed their appetite. A family of swans were slowly moving into the distance, melting into the white carpeted background; it was magic. The appearance of a robin hopping about, its red breast vivid against the white snow. Its cheeky movement and friendliness makes him a welcoming sight in the falling snow and brings a smile to my face.

Winter Magic

18

SUMMER '95

A gentle push on the pole, and the punt drifted the water, easing its way through the overhanging willows. Birches, with their silvery white trunks and long thin branches, were reaching out from the river bank. Bulrushes with their brown heads, tall reeds, intermingled with irises with yellow flowers, all lined the river bank, gently moving in time with the swell of the water. Large dragonflies, electric blue in colour, zipping, whipping here and there, disappearing and returning not knowing which reed to settle on. An assortment of moving colours seemingly tangled up in the shapes of butterflies dancing, zigzagging amongst the reeds and yellow irises around the water's edge. A solitary grebe, with its thin red bill, crest in black and a white front, disappeared beneath the surface of the water. A long pike, green in colour, with a speckled back, its turned-up jaws waiting to snatch a meal, lay motionless in the dark and dapple shade of the reeds. Carp were slowly nosing the riverbed, gently rising to break the surface; the slurping of the water and fins on their back, causing ripples around them. The grebe pops up and looks around, swallows its catch and then disappears again. A white swan flies in, wings outstretched, flip, flaps the surface of the water as it touches down, rearranges its ruffled feathers and silently glides away. "It was magic."

Lazily watching the sun glistening off the overhanging willows and then bouncing the reflection off the water, was all part of drifting the river. Reminiscing about people, places shared and summer days; feeling the water trickle around my fingers was so relaxing.

Suddenly a voice shouted, "You two, time's up!"

19

AGGIE

Aggie pulled her front door shut, making sure she heard it lock. She moved slowly down her path, kicking away the sweet papers and crisp bags as she came across them, wondering why they always ended up in her garden. She then closed the gate behind her.

Her rheumatism was once again playing up making walking slow and at times painful. She had to go out once a week for her pension and bit of shopping.

By the time she arrived at the post office there was a queue as usual. She finally reached the counter and collected her pension. As she was leaving, she heard a commotion. Looking back, she noticed two youths messing about. Aggie carried on going, tutting as she went.

Having got her shopping, Aggie decided to buy her first lottery ticket. Getting in the queue she noticed the youths from the post office at the front buying tickets. Shuffling her way to the counter she finally bought her ticket.

On leaving the shop, Aggie noticed the youths hanging about. Taking no more notice Aggie started making her way home slowly.

As she rounded the corner of her street, the two youths approached, blocking the way. She immediately recognised them from the shops and the post office. They demanded her bags and pushed her. In her anger she threw the bags on the ground spilling the contents everywhere. The youths immediately bent down to pick up what they wanted. As they did, Aggie pushed them over making them get entangled with each other.

At that point a neighbour came running out shouting. As soon as the youths noticed him, they ran off.

Aggie and her neighbour picked up her scattered belongings. Collecting up the shopping and her lottery tickets, he placed them in her bag.

After a few days' rest, she felt slightly better from the shock of the mugging.

Saturday evening soon came round. She sat down in front of her open fire staring at the flames leaping up amongst the burning coals, tears slowly moving down her cheeks, wondering if she could move away from the area. Realizing she could never afford it, she started to cry.

Aggie switched the television on hoping to take her mind off it. She decided to wait for the lottery numbers. Reaching across the armchair for her handbag she fumbled for her ticket. There were three tickets! All she could think, was that in the mugging, the youths had dropped their own tickets and the neighbour, thinking they were Aggie's, had placed them in her bag. She smiled to herself wondering if one of them could be a winner. As the numbers appeared she ticked them off,

12.15.22.5.25.1.

LANE

A grey mist, still lingering around the fields, welcomed me as I turned into the lane with Jack. The coldness of the morning was so fresh, and mixed well with the smell of new-mown grass rising slowly to greet me. Feeling the warmth of the sun on my face, and the coldness of the morning, was so enjoyable. The sun's rays pierced the last of the slowly rising mist and played hide-and-seek behind old willows, distorted with age. Along the grass verge, droplets of dew still covering the grass, formed a carpet of twinkling light under the sun.

Suddenly my eyes caught the wild flowers, scattered along the lane being picked out by the sun. Amongst the coarse grass and last year's dead teasels, with their black seed heads, yellow buttercups just woken up by the sun; too late! I've picked them. Tall, thin, shaking grass gently living up to its name; one or two won't go amiss.

Silently soaring, a skylark breaks the quietness of the morning with its song and welcomes the day. A white dog rose with dew still on its leaves pushes its way through the hedge; smells nice, looks nice, snap! Goes nice with the rest.

Further along the lane the sun was picking out a sprinkling of scarlet poppies, just too nice to pick. Oh well just one.

What's that smell? Honeysuckle, so sweetly scented in the morning. Can just reach it. Snap mmm . . . lovely.

A short walk from the poppies a cluster of mallow, mauve in colour; my favourite wild flower. Must have some to complete the wild bunch.

Looking at my timepiece in a timeless world brought me back to reality.

I suddenly realized I was late for work again.

CHRISTMAS '94

Now where's that sticky tape? Another Christmas present nearly wrapped up. Just a few more to do; another glass of Christmas cheers. "Hic" that's the sixth one.

Granddad's slippers and long johns to do now. I hope I got the right size and colour. Where's that pen? I'll put the label on later, when I find it. A new bag for Jane, to carry her books and pens to school in. Where's my "hic" drink and mince pie? I hope Jane likes the bag. Still can't find the pen. I'll write the tag out later.

Sitting here on the mat, in front of a glowing fire. Christmas presents, tags, wrapping paper, bottle of sherry, a plate of hot mince pies, box of chocolates. "Hic" another bottle of sherry. Christmas tree seems to be swaying. "Hic" good job I got the presents in June. That TV shopping channel is a good idea. "Hic" no pushing and shoving, no parking problems, good selections of presents for everyone.

Where's that bottle? "Hic" there's the pen. I'll write the labels now. "Hic" which label goes on what present? "Hic" I'd like to see their faces, "hic" if the tags get mixed up, "hic". Granddad with a new bag. Jane in long johns and slippers. Christmas tree "is" moving. "Hic" I think!

HAPPY CHRISTMAS EVERYONE.

24

DOLL

Jill would look in the window every time she passed the antique shop. One day she spotted a very old doll in the shop. The price was out of her reach but did not stop her from looking.

For at least three months the doll looked out of the window with no buyers in sight. Jill decided to see if she could buy it. She went inside the shop; it was dark and musty.

After a little while, the owner appeared. He was a man in his late fifties with shifty eyes. Jill became frightened of his appearance. He asked her what she wanted. She told him she was interested in the doll but she had very little money to buy it. She asked if she could pay off for it. He looked at her and told her not to waste his time. She got very upset at his remark, telling the man she liked the doll and would pay as much as she could for it. He just turned away and told her to get out of the shop. At the same time he told her he had an appointment and that he did not have time to discuss the doll.

She left in tears going straight to her grandparents, telling them the sad story. They tried to console her by cuddling and kissing her, telling her not to worry. It made no difference, she was very upset.

Granddad disappeared for a while; Nan slowly calmed her down with sweets and lemonade.

Granddad had been up in the attic. When he appeared he had an old dusty box. Jill looked up from her nan's lap. He opened the box to reveal an old doll just like the one in the shop. She jumped up and ran to him with tears of joy in her eyes. He gave her the doll; a big smile came to her face. There was the same doll she had seen in the shop. It had been in the attic since her grandmother was a little girl.

Just at that moment the door bell rang. Granddad opened the door to reveal the man from the antique shop. He had come to keep his appointment. Granddad told him he had changed his mind about selling some of his antiques, also that he was giving his granddaughter the doll for her eighth birthday; that would be on Sunday.

INSIGHT

Swallows, with their forked tails, acrobatically skimming the surface of the water, catching their unsuspecting meal. The toad surfaces, his large and ever-ready mouth and beady eyes focusing on everything that moves. In a flash, he's gone, his long legs propelling him down, disturbing the debris as he goes. Like miniature dragons, crested newts scavenge as they scurry among the decaying matter.

Above, water boatmen race across the surface like some Olympic oarsmen, unaware that they could be next on the menu. The mayfly just emerging from its chrysalis, stretching its wings straightening its long blue body; his body catching the feel of life, slowly crawling up to the top of the reed; another one possibly for the à la carte menu. As the water warms up, a carp jumps out of its silent world creating ripples across its universe.

Placing a wriggling meal upon the hook, hoping to take that big green fish from the depths of its tranquil world, a voice shouts out

"Can't you read? 'NO FISHING'!"

27

IVY

Ivy had put the telephone down for the umpteenth time in as many days. Trying to get the local council to come and repair some of the damage done to her home, was like getting blood out of a stone. The damage was done when someone had broken in, while she was out shopping. She had discovered the break-in on her return; as she put the key in her door, she knew something was wrong. There were drawers hanging out of the sideboard; papers had been thrown about in the intruder's hurry to find something of value; cash or gold. They had damaged some furniture, plus a window in the back door was broken. As she went into the passage, the thief ran out of the back door fast. This all happened about eight months ago.

Slowly she was coming to terms that the thief would not get caught and sentenced.

Some miles away at a sports stadium, a local lad was being cheered on to the finishing line. One of many he had won over the last two years. He liked the feel of the applause and being noticed. He was hoping to make the international team with his performance that day. He was in good shape and his times were good.

Three weeks later, he received the letter he had hoped for, inviting him to join the team to represent his country. It would be at least four months before he would travel abroad. Then he would be away two months at least, doing what he liked best, running.

He decided to do one more break-in, one week before going abroad; that way no one would suspect him. He had no qualms about going back to the same house he had done before.

The months soon went by; he decided to go one afternoon. When he arrived at the house, the back door was ajar. Seeing no one about, he went in, slowly closing the door behind him. Not hearing anyone, he went upstairs slowly and quietly. He went into the main bedroom, going through the drawers and cupboard, looking for cash.

All of a sudden there was a knock at the front door. In his panic to get out of the house, his foot got caught in some frayed carpet at the top of the stairs. At the same time, he reached for the handrail which came away from the wall, causing him to fall down the staircase with a mighty bang and crash. Next thing he was screaming with pain. He had broken his arm and both his legs.

Ivy came out of the loo; having been working in the garden, the cold always made her go. Ivy made her way down the stairs slowly, looking at the crumpled intruder at the bottom. A smile came to her face as she opened the front door to find two workmen from the council standing there in their overalls. "We've come to repair your handrail, love."

It was Ivy's lucky day. Her handrail was mended, plus the intruder was caught and sentenced, never to "leg it" again.

LYNN

Lynn got up for the fourth time that night, to see to her baby. He seemed to be constantly crying for some reason. The long nights were beginning to tell on her; tiredness and becoming irritable was showing.

She had named her son Jamie. He had been born after a brief affair that summer. The father had washed his hands of the responsibility for the child.

Lynn lived with her mother and three young brothers. Their father had died some years earlier. They lived about eight miles outside of the nearest town. With no car in the family they relied on the local buses to get them about.

The family was already living on the poverty line before the baby came along. Things did get hard for the family; food, nappies, clothes, attending to his needs. As soon as her mum knew she was pregnant, she told Lynn to have an abortion as there was no way they could begin to afford another mouth to feed.

At the time; Lynn insisted she had the baby, but slowly she was regretting having Jamie. Sleepless nights, rowing with her mum, struggling to provide for Jamie, was beginning to tell on her. Reluctantly she began to think of adoption, hoping it would give him a better start in life. To add to their misery, a letter arrived from their new landlord informing them their rent would be going up another six pounds a week from the first of the month. They knew they could not afford it.

Lynn telephoned the landlord. When the man answered, he had a strong Northern dialect which was unusual for the area they lived in. She also detected a slight stammer in his speech. Lynn explained that they could not afford the increase on the rent owing to the fact, she and her mother could not get work on the fields, and that she had a new baby to feed. He was totally uncompromising with her problem, advising her in no uncertain way to vacate the property as soon as possible. As she put the phone down, tears ran down her face, his voice still ringing in her ears, about getting out of their home.

After a lot of heart-searching and tears, Lynn decided to have Jamie adopted. She contacted an agency for the adoption. There was no shortage of couples who wanted a child.

Lynn and her mum also decided to move away once Jamie had been adopted. While the adoption was going through, they both started to clear the house out, going through their home, turning out cupboards and drawers. Lynn came across an old shoe box with the family papers in it. Looking through the contents, she found old gas bills, birth certificates, bits of paper, and receipts. Lynn decided to put the box to one side for her mum to go through later.

Slowly the packing and cleaning was coming to an end; it would be completed by the time Jamie had been adopted.

As the day grew near, for the adoption, Lynn was finding it hard to sleep and eat with the worry, wondering if Jamie was going to a good home.

On the day of the adoption, Lynn got up early to make the most of her last few hours with her son, kissing him, touching him constantly, more than ever. She dressed him in a new blue coat and matching hat from his grandmother, making Jamie look so lovely and cuddly. Lynn made her way down the lane. She had decided to carry Jamie so she could treasure the last few hours before having to give him up.

As she arrived at the bus stop, the postman nodded as he went up the lane. She acknowledged him with a weak smile, her thoughts were with Jamie.

She arrived on time for the adoption. As she entered the room with her son, she nodded to the couple sitting opposite; Jamie's future adoptive parents. She sat down slowly, still wondering if this was the right thing to do.

Lynn was introduced to the couple. The wife did all the talking for the first twenty minutes. Then the husband started. Lynn's ears pricked up, it was the same voice she had heard on the telephone; the same person with no compassion, no feeling of humanity; it was her new landlord. She knew then, that she could not go through with the adoption.

Lynn got up without a word and left the meeting. Her mind was made up, Jamie was staying with her.

As Lynn walked the last hundred yards or so up the lane, her mum came running out of the house, shouting and screaming with joy, to see Lynn and Jamie together. She hugged them both, tears running everywhere. Then she showed Lynn the Premium Bond for £25,000 which the postman had delivered that morning.

CHRISTMAS '95

Still can't find those labels. "Hic." Where's that other bottle of sherry? Must be in the kitchen. "Hic." Christmas tree is still moving from side to side, and the fairy at the top keeps smiling at me. There's the bottle on the table. More mince pies. "Ouch" they're hot. "Hic." I wish the jelly would stop wobbling, I am beginning to feel sick. The trifle looks lovely; red jelly, peaches and all topped with Angel Delight. "Hic." I'll stick my finger in for a quick taste. "Nice." Made a mess of the trifle now. Christmas pudding smells strong. Can't wait to set it alight. Where's those matches? This sherry is nice. "Hic." While I'm in the kitchen, I'll stuff the turkey. "Hic." Why doesn't it keep still? "Oops." Better pick it up off the floor quick. This sherry is going down a treat. Don't like putting my hand inside. Here goes. What's this, labels inside the turkey? Where's that other bottle?

Suddenly a voice shouted out, "Get out of the kitchen love."

HEDGEROW

The fresh stillness of the early morning is slowly creeping in and mingling with the musky smell of dampness left by night. Blackbirds, perched high, singing softly, welcome the sun, slowly peering over the hedgerow and opening up the day. Its rays gently piercing the rising mist and getting caught on droplets of dew and winking. The sunlight beginning to catch the night dew still clinging to cobwebs woven like "old lady's lace" into the hedgerow, like strings of pearls not yet broken.

Below the hedgerow, patterned with white lace, a bushy red tail disappears through a well-worn path, till night once again.

On the dewed lawn, a speckled thrush, pulling hard on one end, the other end trying harder to stay in the ground. Nearby, miniature daffodils, bright yellow in the early light, reveal themselves as the sun embraces them, on a par with gold nuggets.

Droplets of dew, slowly rolling to the edge of the leaves of a wild campion, splash to the ground missing the large green slugs slithering and sliming their way back to their unmarked stones after a night of destruction.

A pheasant appears from beneath the hedgerow; its bright plumage catching the early sun as it runs across the dewed lawn, leaving its presence.

Suddenly, crunch, crunch, hobnail boots come crashing in; it's the milkman. The world arrives!

34

BREAKFAST

A robin flies over the hedge with its breakfast and settles on a sundial. The early sun catches him watching the events patiently around the garden. Behind a limp and shredded hosta, still coated in dew, a thrush taps out a tune on a shell — tap, tap, much to the annoyance of the occupier whose fate is sealed. Along the gravel path, borders of flowers slowly opening and coming into colours as the sun warms them up; bumblebees taking advantage of the opening and popping in for pollen. Across the garden at the edge of the pond, reflection of a rod and line dangling in the water goes unnoticed by the owner with a cracked smile and red hat, who's stone dead. A blackbird flies out "low" from a honeysuckle cascading down from an old broken trellis, its sweet scent seeping across the garden. On the lawn, starlings picking and probing amongst the wormcrusts of the night, making their way across the wet lawn for breakfast.

Suddenly a cat appears and breakfast is over.

JOURNEY

We got up as usual on Wednesday morning; had our usual breakfast; bowl of cornflakes, cup of tea and toast. Sitting there talking and thinking about what to do for the day.

The sun was already up and shining; the day was starting well. We decided to go out for the day, after we had done our jobs washing-up, making the beds, generally tidying up the place. Watering the flower tubs and hanging baskets; so much colour about. Fed the fish in the pond, put the dust bags out for the dustmen before we went out.

I had been driving for about an hour. The countryside was looking nice; new leaves on the trees and the hedgerows were turning green.

All of a sudden we saw one hiding behind a hedge. "I do not like them," I said, turning to my wife. She agreed.

Few more miles along the road we saw some more. Some were standing on the pavement, others were still hiding around the back. One old lady was fighting to put one out. She managed it after a struggle.

As we travelled along, wild poppies were mixed with wild flowers, creating a wonderful splash of colour along the lanes. As we neared a town, we could see them again standing outside gates and at the end of paths. Some children were playing hide-and-seek around them; their mums telling them to come away from them at once. An old man was complaining to his neighbour about them. It made no difference, he was stuck with one. As we went through the town they seemed to be watching us go by.

As the day went on, we were enjoying the colour of the countryside. Some of the fields were a bright yellow having been planted with rape seed. We stopped at a pub for a drink and something to eat. We were there about an hour and a half. We enjoyed our meal. As we pulled out of the car park we spotted three of them chained up against the back wall near the kitchen. We decided to make our way home having had a nice day out. We had enjoyed the meal and ride.

When we got home, the dustmen had taken our rubbish bag. Having seen those larger dustbins on wheels during the day, with people struggling to put them out, then trying to hide them when they had been emptied, we were both glad we did not have a

WHEELIE BIN.

YOURS

Take my hand, it's yours to touch.
Take my arms, they're yours to shelter.
Take my ears, they're yours for whispering.
Take my eyes, they're yours to tell me.
Take my face, the smile is yours.
Take my heart, it's full of love.
Take me, I'm yours.